ARTHUR
Jumps into Fall

by Marc Brown

LITTLE, BROWN AND COMPANY

New York ❧ Boston ❧ London

Arthur and D.W. were finishing their breakfast.
"I have a job for you today, Arthur," said Dad.
"I want you to rake leaves in the backyard."

"Wouldn't today be a good time for D.W. to learn to rake?"
Arthur asked.

Dad shook his head. "D.W. will be helping me with other things."

Arthur looked up at the empty tree.
"This is all your fault," he said.
Then he started to rake.

The leaves seemed to be sticking to the ground.
Arthur raked harder.

Pretty soon he had made a little pile of leaves.

"What do you think, Pal?" he asked.
Pal took a sniff. Then he picked up a leaf in his mouth
and added it to the pile.

Arthur kept raking.
The pile got a little bigger.
"This is a lot of work," he said to Pal.
"Maybe we should take a break."

Arthur and Pal jumped in the pile of leaves. Then they jumped again and again.
Pretty soon the leaves were scattered all over the yard again.

"Arthur, what are you doing?" asked Francine. She walked
up with Buster and the Brain.
"I'm raking," said Arthur.
"You're not doing a very good job," said the Brain.
"It's a question of applying force properly. Here, let me show you."

The Brain started raking.
"See how I bend my elbows?" he said.
"I do," said Arthur. "Show me more."

Now Francine took a turn. "This isn't so hard," she said.
"All it takes is organization and muscle power."

"Wow!" said Buster. "This could be the biggest pile of leaves in the country—or maybe the whole world."

Finally, all the leaves were collected. "You see?" said the Brain.
"That's how it's done."
Arthur nodded. "Thanks, everyone. It's perfect."

"Just perfect!"